Troll
Bowl

Cat
Hat

Mop
Hop

Humpty
Dumpty

Bears
Stairs

Big
Pig

Fairy
Cherry

Elf
Shelf

Owl
Towel

Fish
Dish

Socks
Blocks

Mouse
Blouse

Fed
Bed

Toad
Road

Man
Fan

For Mom and Dad
—AM

For Theo and Gus
—AH

Acknowledgments

From the author: Special thanks to Mary-Kate Gaudet, Regan Winter, Rotem Moscovich, Heather Crowley, Stephanie Lurie, Steven Malk, Arik Cohen, David Ebert, and Cirocco Dunlap.

From the illustrator: Special thanks to Véronique Lefèvre Sweet, Elena Giovinazzo, Robin Rosenthal, Stacey Sperling, and Ruvane Shapiro.

About This Book

The illustrations for this book were done in gouache and colored pencil on watercolor paper. This book was edited by Mary-Kate Gaudet and designed by Véronique Lefèvre Sweet. The production was supervised by Patricia Alvarado, and the production editor was Marisa Finkelstein. The body text was set in Mrs Eaves Roman, the speech balloons were set in the author's hand-lettered font, and the display type is HenHouse AOE Regular.

CHESTER VAN CHIME
Who Forgot How to RHYME

by Avery Monsen • Illustrated by Abby Hanlon

Little, Brown and Company
New York Boston

There once was a youngster named Chester van Chime, who woke up one day and forgot how to rhyme.

It baffled poor Chester. He felt almost queasy.
To match up two sounds, it was always so...

...simple for him.

See, Chester loved rhyming, in poem or song.
It always felt right, but today it felt...

...not right. VERY not right.

He tried not to panic. He played it real cool and picked up his backpack and walked to his…

SHOE ZOO

SCHOOL POOL!

...learning place with teachers and stuff.

He walked past the butcher and walked past the baker.
He passed Mr. Waxler, the candlestick...

. . .guy.

In class, Mrs. Stevens knew something was wrong when Chester could not sing the words of a...

...very popular nursery rhyme.

"The itsy-bitsy spider climbed up the waterspout.
Down came the rain and washed the spider..."

...right onto the floor, totally ruining his day.

His friends tried to help tackle Chester's complaint.
They made him three rhymes with some paper and...

...assorted art supplies.

The dog jumped over the...

Sideways tree?

The goat rowed the...

Canoe?

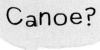

The bear combed his...

Silky-smooth brown fur?!

Things weren't looking good, but they didn't despair.
They sat Chester down in a velvety…

...seat.

Then they brought *tons* of rhymes to the room where he sat.

Muddy foot wipe.

Fancy-pants head cover.

Extra big, mousy-lookin' dude.

And they made *all* the rhymes they could possibly make.

Very sad cow.

The crystal-clear waters of Winnipesaukee, the third largest swimmin' hole in New England.

But none of it worked. Chester still couldn't rhyme.
He felt like a clock that could not tell the...

...hours or seconds or anything!

He slowly walked home, and he shuffled his feet...

...past Waxler, the baker, and the guy who chops...
all-natural hickory-smoked bacon.

They each had a job, and they did it with glee.
If he couldn't rhyme, well then who would he…

…turn into?

But suddenly something popped into his head.
That baker had probably baked some bad…

…sourdough.

The butcher and candle man both made mistakes,
Like badly dipped candles or poorly sliced…

…brisket.

"We all have bad days!" Chester said with a grin.
"And rhymes aren't a contest to lose or to...

...come in first place!"

"So maybe I don't need to be quite so stressed
if I give it my all but I'm not at my…

…tippy-top peak performance."

And, easy as that, Chester's problem was done
when he realized that playing with words should be...

As the sun turned to red and the moon started climbing, young Chester could not stop his smile.

Or his rhyming.

Moose
Goose

Balloon
Moon
Spoon

Fat
Cat

Duck
Truck

Shell
Bell

Pig
Dig

Book
Hook

Pen
Hen

Mice
Dice

Barn
Yarn

Pail
Whale

Blue
Shoe

Bat
Mat

Face
Vase

Sleep
Sheep

Bee
Tree

Vest
Nest